THIS WALT DISNEY CLASSIC EDITION
BELONGS TO:

Copyright © 2001 by Disney Enterprises, Inc.

For information address
Disney Editions,
114 Fifth Avenue,
New York, New York 10011-5690

Produced by:
Welcome Enterprises, Inc.
588 Broadway, Suite 303
New York, New York 10012

ISBN 0-7868-5352-2

Library of Congress Cataloging-in-Publication Data on file.

Printed in China by Toppan

FIRST EDITION

1 3 5 7 9 10 8 6 4 2

Walt Disney's
Babes in Toyland

Story adapted by Monique Peterson
Illustrations by The Walt Disney Studio
Adapted by Earl and Carol Marshall

A Welcome Book

EDITIONS

New York

One day, Mary Contrary found a poster
from the Toymaker in Toyland. It read:

WANTED: HELPER TO MAKE TOYS. URGENT.

So Mary, her friend Tom Piper, and her younger brothers and sisters wandered along the edge of the Forest of No Return in search of Toyland. Wee Willie Winkie stopped to ask the trees if they knew where the Toymaker lived. But all they did was shake their leaves and rattle their branches.

Finally, they came to a clearing. "I think we've found it," said Tom.

Underneath their feet, the grass gave way to a stone path lined with scented wildflowers. Across the bridge the children heard the welcoming *ta-ta-ta* of the toy soldiers' trumpets.

Boy Blue had never seen such a spectacular sight. "Look, Bo-Peep—ice-cream-cone towers and candy-cane columns. Do you think they're good enough to eat?"

"There's only one way to find out—let's go!"

They ran past the clowns and the blocks marked *T*, past the toy-soldier guards, and the golden flagpole with the Toyland flag flying in the breeze.

From the front steps of the great door, the Toymaker's floppy-eared watchdog lifted his head and let out a *ruff-ruff-ruff!*

But by the time they reached the front door, everything seemed strangely quiet. The soldiers had stopped trumpeting, the dog stopped barking, even the birds stopped singing. The sign on the door told them everything they needed to know. "Perhaps he doesn't need our help, after all," sighed Mary.

TOYLAND TOY FACTORY
CLOSED
for
ALTERATIONS
business
is not as usual
GENIUS AT WORK
INSIDE

Meanwhile, deep inside the Toy Factory, the Toymaker was hard at work worrying because he didn't have any toys.

"Your troubles will soon be over," his assistant, Grumio, reassured him. "My new invention will put Toyland back in business."

"Well . . . er . . . all right," the Toymaker finally agreed. "I suppose it can't hurt to take a peek."

"From this point forward, you can forget about drawing plans, or painting faces, or tightening screws, or hammering nails," announced Grumio.

"Have you found someone to help us?" asked the Toymaker.

"We won't need anyone's help—my fabulous toy-making machine will do it all!" Grumio declared.

The *tick-tock, tick-tock* of the clock echoed against the walls of the large room.

"Oh, my goodness!" moaned the Toymaker. "It's half past October. That gives us—"

"Exactly two and a half months until Christmas," grinned Grumio. "More than enough time."

The Toymaker raised his eyebrow. "Are you sure?"

"I'm absolutely, positively certain," Grumio assured him.

"My latest concept in automation will totally amaze you," Grumio said eagerly.

"Hmm." The Toymaker rubbed his chin, thinking about all of his poor assistant's half-baked ideas. Grumio was so much better at making messes than making machines.

"Here's the moment you've been waiting for!" cheered Grumio, yanking the big blue cover away.

"Just wait until you see this." Grumio smiled as he reached into his pocket. He pulled out some yellow string, a bit of lace, a strand of ribbon, and a bow.

START

"I simply toss these items into my marvelous toy-making machine . . . add a dash of sugar and a little bit of spice . . . and pull the *Start* switch."

The engine churned,
the wheels turned. The
machine sputtered and rattled
and hummed and drummed.

Then, in no time at all . . . out popped a perfectly made doll.
"Remarkable!" exclaimed the Toymaker. "Grumio, this is
simply astonishing! Now it looks like we'll be able to make our
Christmas deadline after all."

"That's only the beginning,"
said Grumio. One by one, he
dropped bits of this and dabs of
that into his machine . . .

And out came dollhouses
with pink window shades,
and floppy clowns for circus parades,

wind-up mice with fuzzy felt ears,

balls, and bats for baseball cheers,

many a jigsaw puzzle piece,

party hats with
feathers and fleece,

every letter of the alphabet,

and a supersonic rocket jet.

"Grumio, you're a genius!" cheered the Toymaker.
Grumio beamed.

The Toymaker decorated his assistant with ribbons and badges. "You shall be Toyland's most honored citizen."

"Mmm-hmm." Grumio swelled with pride.

"And we'll make millions of trinkets and bears, drums and dolls, ships and . . ."

"Yes." Grumio smiled proudly, agreeing with everything the Toymaker said.

GIRLS TOYS

"... and balls and blocks and railroad trains!" The Toymaker dashed to the machine, bursting with ideas. He pulled every lever, flipped every switch, pushed every button, twisted every knob, and turned every crank. Down the chute he tossed springs and bolts, jars of paint, patterns and plans, ribbons and lace.

Lights started flashing, wheels started spinning, and bells started ringing.

But Grumio was too busy counting his awards to notice what the Toymaker was doing.

Suddenly the machine's horns started honking and sirens started blaring.

"Wait!" Grumio shouted.

"Mr. Toymaker, you're overloading it, sir! You can only make one toy at a time."

But Grumio's warning came too late.

The big toy-making machine began to sputter. It began to hiss.

Then it began to spit nuts and bolts and springs and bits. Lightbulbs burst and set off sparks. Then . . .

SLOW FAST

...KABOOM!

The room filled with a cloud of thick, black smoke.

Then the machine started to cough, and it started to wheeze.

Finally it let out a great, big gasp and collapsed into a pile of broken pieces.

Meanwhile, at the edge of Toyland, Tom, Mary, and all her brothers and sisters had given up hope of helping the Toymaker. Sadly they trod toward the Forest of No Return. But the toy-making machine's powerful explosion shook the entire land.

"The Toymaker really *does* need our help!" cried Mary. The children ran back across the cobblestone bridge *clippety*, *clippety*, *clippety*, past the toy-soldier guards, and past the Toyland flagpole. The front door swung wide open and welcomed the children inside.

They ran toward the wailing sounds of the sobbing Toymaker. "Whatever will I do now?" he cried.

"We've come to help," explained Tom. "We've come all the way from Mother Goose Village, where we saw your poster."

"What! Children?" declared the Toymaker. "I can't possibly allow you to help me. Don't you know that children should never be allowed to see toys before Christmas?"

"But if we don't help you, there won't be any toys at all this year," said Mary.

The Toymaker scratched his head and thought for a moment. "Hmm, I suppose you're right." He nodded. "Then let's get started . . . time's a-wasting!"

So the Toymaker whisked the children away to every corner of the factory where he kept all his toy parts, paints, and secret supplies.

Little Boy Blue discovered mountains of buttons and sewed them on teddy bears for noses and eyes.

Wee Willie Winkie sang lullaby songs as he tacked the rockers onto rocking horses and chairs.

Bo-Peep took baskets of thread and sewed doll clothes, and puppets, and beanbag toys.

Tom found boxes of every size and shape for every finished toy.

Mary wrapped the gifts in brightly colored paper and festive silk bows.

The Toymaker, happier than ever, put the finishing touches on every last present. He attached handwritten cards that read:

DON'T OPEN TILL CHRISTMAS.

And when all the work was done, Grumio came out with his best invention of all—hand-picked, hand-squeezed, Pink Lemonade Supreme.

"I made these from the finest pink lemons Toyland has to offer." Grumio smiled as he poured glasses of the delicious drink for everyone.

COLLECT ALL THESE!